I CAN READ ABOUT

TRUCKS
AND
CARS

Written by Norman Olson

Illustrated by Steven Smith

Troll Associates

The very first trucks and cars were funny looking.

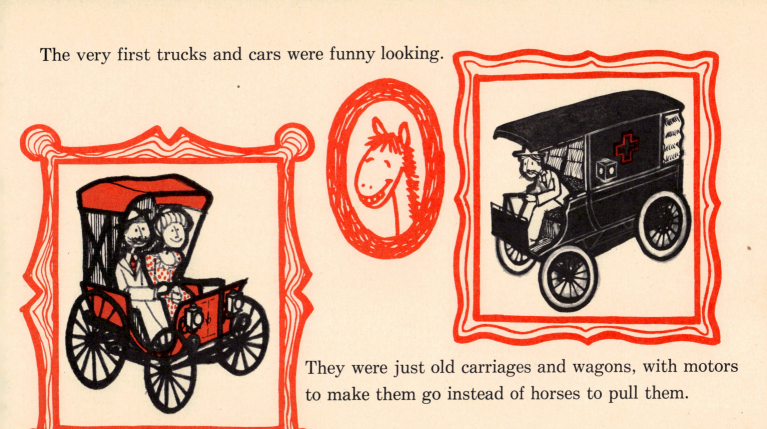

They were just old carriages and wagons, with motors to make them go instead of horses to pull them.

Most people didn't like these "horseless carriages."
They puffed out big, black clouds of smoke and
made lots of noise, which scared horses.

The brave people who drove these first cars and trucks
had many problems. Their cars often broke down,
and people would shout "Get a horse!"—and laugh at them.

Drivers had to wear goggles to protect their eyes from dirt and pebbles.

Roads were full of mudholes and deep ruts, and gas stations were many miles apart.

GAS STATION
10 MILES →

Today, millions of trucks and cars zip along on concrete highways.
How different they look from the old-fashioned horseless carriages!
Our modern cars are lower and longer, and the trucks are
much larger and stronger.

The biggest truck you'll see on the highway is the TRACTOR-TRAILER. The driver sits up front in the tractor part. Behind, in the trailer part, is the truck's cargo.

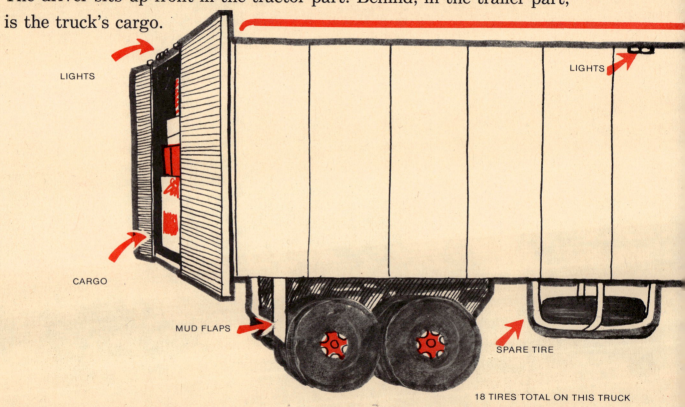

LIGHTS

LIGHTS

CARGO

MUD FLAPS

SPARE TIRE

18 TIRES TOTAL ON THIS TRUCK

Cargo is the name for things the truck is carrying.

TRAILER OR RIG

EXHAUST OR MUFFLER

LIGHTS

HORN

LIGHT

REFRIGERATOR BOX

AIR VENT

SLEEPER CAB

REFLECTORS

MUD FLAPS

DOLLY WHEELS

TRACTOR

Truck drivers call a
tractor-trailer a RIG.
It can carry anything
from pigs to parachutes!

Some rigs are big
refrigerators on wheels.
They bring fresh meats,
vegetables and fruits
to market.

Other rigs, called MOVING VANS,
carry people's furniture
when they move to a new town.

Still other rigs are filled with
books, bicycles, clothes and toys—
and all the things you buy in
department stores.

A TANKER is a special kind of rig, like a great big bottle on wheels. Tankers bring gasoline from the refinery to the gas station. Other tankers carry milk from the farm to the milk plant, where it is put into bottles and cartons.

The FLAT-BED TRAILER has a long, flat trailer with no sides or roof. Often, it is used to carry logs from the forest to the sawmill.

A LOADER has a big scoop up front
to pick up dirt and rocks.
Its large wheels help the loader
ride over bumpy ground
      and through mud.

A SNOWPLOW uses its scoop to push snow
off roads and highways and make them safe
in winter. The snowplow sometimes sprinkles sand
or gravel on the roads to cover slippery ice.

Another truck that helps keep us safe is
the FIRE ENGINE. Firehouses have two kinds
of fire engines. The PUMPER TRUCK
brings the hoses to the fire and pumps the water.

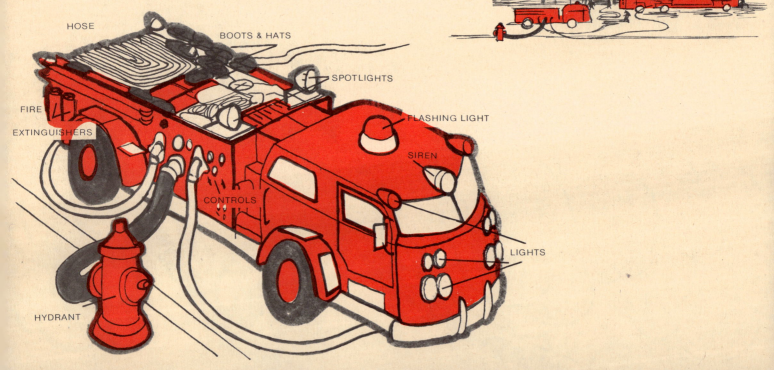

HOSE

BOOTS & HATS

SPOTLIGHTS

FIRE
EXTINGUISHERS

FLASHING LIGHT

SIREN

CONTROLS

LIGHTS

HYDRANT

The other fire engine is the HOOK AND LADDER TRUCK.
It is so long that it needs two drivers—one to steer the front
and one to steer the rear wheels around corners! The tall ladder
helps firemen fight fires in tall buildings.

The DUMP TRUCK carries dirt and rocks.
See how the back tips so that
everything falls out.

Watch out!

The CEMENT-MIXER
brings wet cement
that is needed for building houses
or new sidewalks. The big bucket
on its back keeps turning
so the cement stays soft
until it can be used.

GARBAGE TRUCKS collect trash from your home, your friends' homes, and all the buildings in town, and take it away.

The TOW TRUCK helps people whose cars have broken down or have been in an accident. The big hook and chain on its back are used to pull cars back to the gas station to be fixed.

Small MAIL TRUCKS pick up letters from mail boxes all over town, and take them to the post office.

Big mail trucks sometimes carry the mail from other towns to your town. Then, your mailman can bring you birthday cards and letters from your friends far away.

Many small trucks may come to your home.

If you get a new phone,
the TELEPHONE TRUCK will come.

The milkman delivers milk and cream
in his MILK TRUCK.

Workmen drive small trucks called PICK-UP TRUCKS.

The plumber carries all his tools and equipment in the back of a pick-up truck.

The man from the cleaners delivers clothes in a PANEL TRUCK.

Some trucks are built for very special jobs.

Here's a CAMPER—it's like a small house on wheels.
You can travel to exciting places and then eat and sleep
in the camper. It's fun to go on vacation with a camper truck!

In the summer, your favorite kind of truck is probably
the ICE CREAM TRUCK. You know the ice cream truck is coming
when you hear the jingle of its bell.

Banks use an ARMORED CAR to take money from one bank to another.
An armored car is a small truck made of strong metal,
with thick glass windows. Guards have to make sure
that no one steals the money!

The BOOKMOBILE is a library on wheels.

The bookmobile often visits towns where there is no library.

Does your town have a library?

Another special kind of truck is the
NEW-CAR CARRIER. It carries cars from the factory to the new-car
showroom. A showroom is a place where people can buy new cars.

There are also many special kinds of cars.

The policeman uses his POLICE CAR
to help people in trouble.

The Fire Chief rushes to a fire
in his FIRE CHIEF'S CAR.

When people get very sick,
they sometimes need an AMBULANCE
to take them to the hospital.
An ambulance has special equipment
to help sick people.

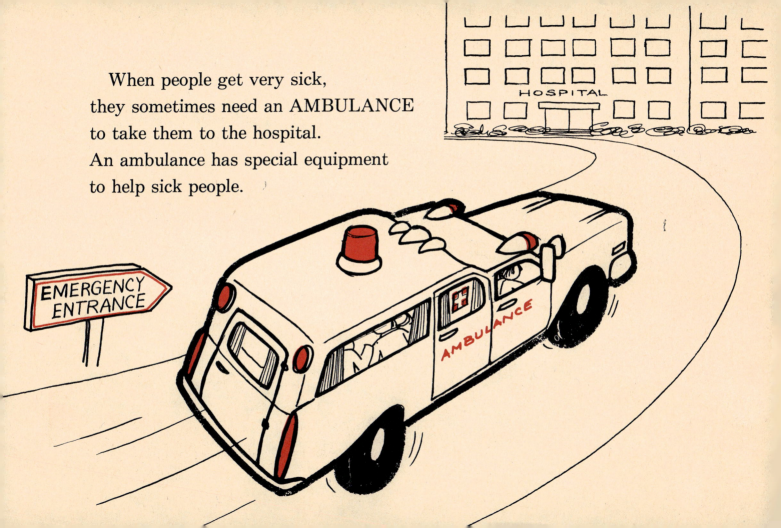

Z-O-O-M! A RACING CAR is a very special kind of car.
Racing car drivers try to find out whose car is fastest.
They drive their cars faster and faster around a road called a race track.

A TAXICAB is a car that takes people around town. If they don't have a car, a taxicab will take them where they want to go.

You can also take a BUS to go from one place to another.

If you live far away from your school, you probably ride in a SCHOOL BUS.
Flashing lights on the bus warn car drivers to be careful.

Cars have many uses.

A car may help your mother bring the groceries
home from the store.

A car may take your father to his job,
or take you for a ride to the seashore.

A car can take you to many exciting places—
to the mountains,
to the zoo,
or to the store to buy something new!

If you could drive a car, where would **you** like to go?

NORTH

WEST

EAST

SOUTH

FUN PARK

ZOO